MANNY MACHADO

BASEBALL SUPERSTAR

BY TODD KORTEMEIER

First Edition
First Printing, 2019

Book design by Jake Nordby
Cover design by Jake Nordby
Photographs ©: Ross D. Franklin/AP Images, cover, 1; Gail Burton/AP Images, 4–5, 7; tome213/Shutterstock Images, 8; Stefano Ember/Shutterstock Images, 10; Brian Bissell/AP Images, 13; Patrick Semansky/AP Images, 14–15; Matt York/AP Images, 17, 27; Chris O'Meara/AP Images, 19; Billy Hurst/AP Images, 20–21; Mark J. Terrill/AP Images, 22–23; Charlie Riedel/AP Images, 25; Red Line Editorial, 29; Ross D. Franklin/AP Images, 30

Press Box Books, an imprint of Press Room Editions.

Library of Congress Control Number: 2019936709

ISBN
978-1-63494-093-1 (library bound)
978-1-63494-094-8 (paperback)
978-1-63494-095-5 (epub)
978-1-63494-096-2 (hosted ebook)

Distributed by North Star Editions, Inc.
2297 Waters Drive
Mendota Heights, MN 55120
www.northstareditions.com

Printed in the United States of America

About the Author

Todd Kortemeier is a sportswriter, editor, and children's book author. A lifelong Padres fan, he is beyond excited for the Manny Machado era. He and his wife live near Minneapolis with their dog.

TABLE OF CONTENTS

1 MANNY MANIA

Manny Machado slipped on his white-and-orange uniform. Then he stepped onto the field. Machado was just 20 years old on August 9, 2012. Yet he was already playing for the Baltimore Orioles. More than 20,000 fans showed up in Baltimore that night to see his Major League Baseball (MLB) debut. It was a huge jump for Machado. The night before, he'd been playing in Double-A. That's two levels below MLB.

Manny Machado connects for a single in his MLB debut.

It didn't take long for him to feel comfortable at the plate. After a ground-out in his first at-bat, he came to bat again in the fifth inning. He fell behind 0–2. But on the next pitch, he laced a hit to deep right-center field. It rolled all the way to the wall, and he cruised into third base for a triple. Machado added a single in the seventh.

The next day, Machado showed off his power. He led off the fifth inning with a solo home run. Then in the next inning, with two runners on, he swung hard. The ball landed deep in the left-field stands for a three-run home run.

HOT CORNER

Machado began his minor league career as a shortstop. The Orioles had other ideas for him. In May 2012, they began teaching him third base. He practiced before games. Over and over again, Machado fielded ground balls. Still, he had played the position in only two minor league games before making his Orioles debut there.

Machado became the youngest Orioles player to hit two home runs in one game.

Machado received a standing ovation as the crowd chanted his name.

"Manny Mania" soon took over Baltimore. But this was only the beginning of his special career.

2 MIAMI MANNY

Manny Machado was born on July 6, 1992. He was born and raised in the United States. However, his family was originally from the Dominican Republic, where baseball was a national obsession. Manny's family brought that passion to Florida.

In Manny's hometown near Miami, Florida, there were all sorts of fun things to do outside. But while Manny's friends liked going to the pool and relaxing on weekends, he headed to the baseball

Manny's hometown of Hialeah is just northwest of Miami, Florida.

Many kids in the Dominican Republic grow up dreaming of making it to the major leagues.

field instead. Manny's uncle Gio Brito would hit him bucket after bucket of balls so he could practice fielding.

Manny's grandfather Francisco Nunez was also a big part of his life. He taught Manny the importance of bunting. He knew his grandson could hit and field well. But he said that truly great players also mastered small details such as bunting.

Manny's mother supported him, too. But Rosa Nunez worked two jobs and rarely got to see Manny play. Manny knew his father growing up, but his father did not live with the family. Rosa raised Manny and his older sister Yasmine alone.

By the time he was a high school senior, Manny was one of the top prospects in baseball. He had an amazing batting average of .639 that year, with 12 home runs and 68 runs batted in (RBIs) in only 29 games.

MIAMI ROOTS

Manny has known some of his friends in MLB since he was a kid in Miami. He grew up near Albert Almora. They are so close that they each consider the other a cousin. Manny is also close with Yonder Alonso. Alonso tried to get Manny to play for the University of Miami. Manny later married Alonso's sister, Yainee.

He had planned to play college baseball at Florida International University. But his plans changed when the Baltimore Orioles chose him third overall in the 2010 MLB draft.

Manny's grandfather did not live to see him become a major league player. He died in 2009. But Rosa was able to see Manny's success. And with part of his $5.25 million signing bonus from the Orioles, Manny bought her a house.

Manny's success continued in the Orioles' organization. He moved through four levels of minor league baseball in 2010 and 2011. By mid-2012, the Orioles felt he was ready. He skipped Triple-A and went straight to the majors.

Manny cruised through the minors, including 38 games with the Class A Delmarva Shorebirds.

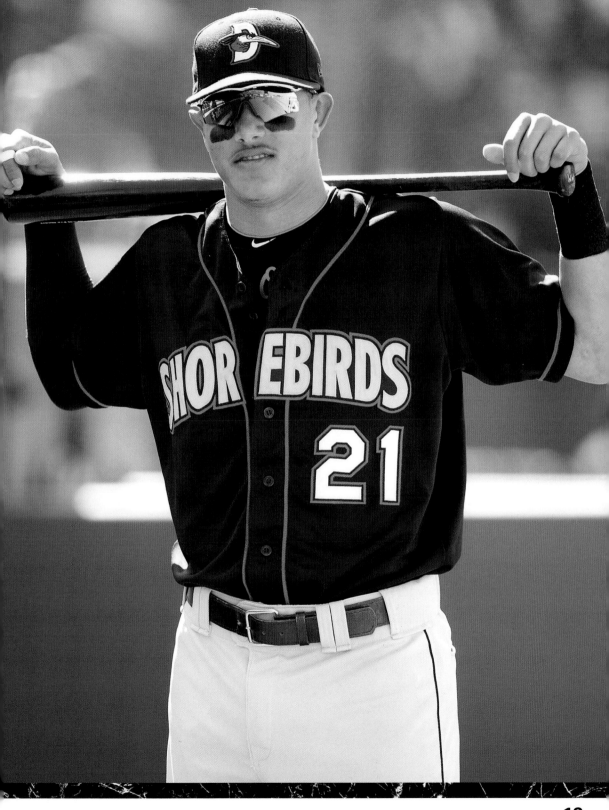

3 BREAKING INTO BIRDLAND

Manny Machado was a good luck charm for the 2012 Orioles. He joined the team in August. That helped boost the Orioles to their first playoff appearance since 1997. Machado went from 20-year-old minor leaguer to playing in the MLB playoffs in just three months.

The Orioles faced the New York Yankees in the divisional round. And Machado showed he was ready for the big stage. Game 3 was at Yankee Stadium in front of 50,000 screaming Yankees fans.

Machado fit right in with the Orioles in 2012.

With the game tied 1–1, Machado stepped to the plate. On the first pitch, he hammered a ball to deep left-center field. His home run gave the Orioles a 2–1 lead. But they went on to lose the game in extra innings. They then lost the series in five games.

Machado started off hot in 2013. He hit .304 in April and .355 in May. He was selected to his first All-Star Game. However, Machado also showed he could have a temper. On June 27, he was called out for swinging at strike three. He argued that he fouled the ball off and should not have struck out. The umpire ejected him from the game.

Great hitting and a hot temper were early themes in Machado's career. Unfortunately, so were injuries. Machado injured his knee in September and had to miss the rest of

Machado won his first Gold Glove at third base in 2013.

the season. Surgery kept him out until the following May. That June, Machado thought an opponent tagged him too hard in a game. He started a fight. MLB responded by suspending Machado for five games. He apologized and said he hoped to learn from the incident. Then injuries struck again. Machado hurt his right knee in August. He missed the rest of the season.

REPRESENTING THE DR

Machado is an American by birth. But in international baseball, he is eligible to represent the Dominican Republic. He chose to play for the Dominican Republic at the 2017 World Baseball Classic. He did it as a tribute to his family. Machado hit .321 in the tournament.

Finally healthy in 2015, Machado put together his best season yet. He hit 35 home runs. That was more than he'd hit in the previous three years combined. He then hit 37 home runs in 2016. He also started his first All-Star Game. But he needed to learn to control his emotions. Machado charged the mound in a June game after being hit by a pitch. He was suspended for four games this time. Still, there was no doubt he was one of the best players in baseball. And at 24, he was still getting better.

Everything was looking up for Machado in 2016.

HEAVY HITTER

Manny Machado hits the ball hard, and he hits it far. That is confirmed by looking at his average launch angle, exit velocity, and hit distance. All three are regularly among the best in baseball. What do those statistics measure?

- Launch angle measures the vertical direction of the ball as it leaves the bat. It ranges from straight out (0 degrees) to straight up (90 degrees). A launch angle of 10 to 25 degrees tends to lead to a line drive.

- Exit velocity measures the speed of the baseball as it comes off the bat. Top hitters tend to average more than 90 miles per hour (145 kmh).

- Hit distance measures how for the ball lands from home plate.

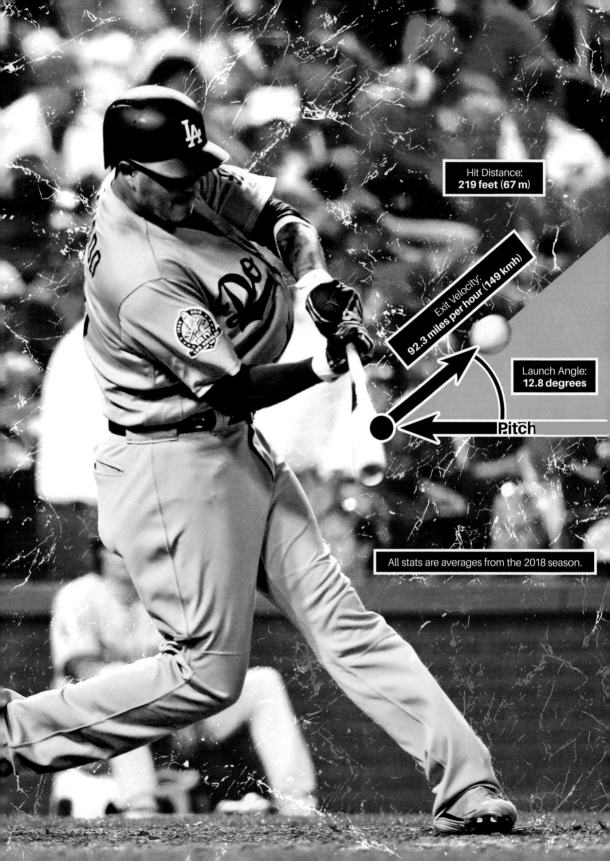

Hit Distance:
219 feet (67 m)

Exit Velocity:
92.3 miles per hour (149 kmh)

Launch Angle:
12.8 degrees

Pitch

All stats are averages from the 2018 season.

4 HEADING WEST

Manny Machado entered the 2018 season on the last year of his contract. Baltimore had become his home. He enjoyed playing there. But he wasn't going to worry about what the future held. And he played like it. In 96 games with the Orioles, Machado hit .315 with 24 home runs. But the Orioles were not winning. In fact, they had not won a single playoff series since 2014. So they traded Machado to the Los Angeles Dodgers.

The Los Angeles Dodgers believed Machado could help them win a World Series.

The Dodgers were the defending National League champs. They were willing to trade some young players for a star like Machado. And with Machado, they went back to the World Series again. But Machado played poorly in his first Fall Classic, hitting .182. Fans also complained that he made some dirty plays.

After the season, Machado had no contract. He was free to sign with any team. Many people thought he would go to the New York Yankees. They were one of the few teams that could afford to sign him.

Machado did indeed sign a huge deal. It was worth $300 million over 10 years. But where he signed shocked everyone. On February 19, 2019, Machado signed with the San Diego Padres. Unlike the Dodgers or Yankees, the Padres had not won much. They

Machado was all smiles when being introduced as the newest member of the Padres.

had never won the World Series. They had not even made the playoffs since 2006.

But the Padres had a lot of young players who were expected to be good very soon. Machado liked the idea of being a team leader. He liked the idea of doing something that had

HELP IS ON THE WAY

Machado provided a big boost to the Padres lineup. In 2018, Machado hit .297 with 37 home runs. In both statistics, he would have led the 2018 Padres by a wide margin. No San Diego player had more than 26 home runs or hit better than .280 in 2018. In fact, only six Padres had hit more than 36 home runs in a season in the team's 50-year history.

not been done before: bringing a championship to San Diego.

Machado was used to being one of the best players on the field. But now he had the pressure of a whole city expecting him to do great things. Machado wasn't worried. He thought it was just the beginning. He was excited to start playing for his new team.

Padres fans were eager to get Machado's big bat in the lineup.

TIMELINE

1. **Hialeah, Florida (1992)**
   Manny Machado is born on July 6.

2. **Secaucus, New Jersey (2010)**
   The Baltimore Orioles select Machado third overall in the MLB draft.

3. **Sarasota, Florida (2010)**
   Machado makes his pro baseball debut with the Gulf Coast League Orioles.

4. **Baltimore, Maryland (2012)**
   Machado makes his MLB debut with the Orioles at Oriole Park at Camden Yards.

5. **Queens, New York (2013)**
   Machado plays in his first MLB All-Star Game, which is held at Citi Field.

6. **Los Angeles, California (2018)**
   Machado is traded to the Los Angeles Dodgers during the All-Star break.

7. **San Diego, California (2019)**
   Machado signs a 10-year, $300-million contract with the San Diego Padres.

MAP

AT-A-GLANCE

Birth date: July 6, 1992

Birthplace: Hialeah, Florida

Position: Third base

Bats: Right

Throws: Right

Size: 6 feet 3 inches, 215 pounds

Current team: San Diego Padres (2019–)

Past teams: Baltimore Orioles (2012–18), Los Angeles Dodgers (2018)

Major awards: MLB All-Star (2013, 2015, 2016, 2018), Gold Glove (2013, 2015)

Accurate through the 2018 season.

GLOSSARY

bonus
A one-time payment a player receives from his team.

bunt
When a player chooses to tap the ball with his bat rather than swing. This is sometimes done to "sacrifice" the hitter and advance the runner.

contract
An agreement between a player and his team that states how much he will be paid and for how long.

debut
A player's first appearance.

draft
A process in which teams choose new players to add to their rosters.

eject
To kick a player out of a game for breaking the rules.

minor league
The lower levels in which pro baseball players develop their skills.

prospect
An up-and-coming player who could someday reach the major leagues.

standing ovation
When people are so impressed by a performance they rise to their feet and cheer.

suspend
To punish a player for a rules violation by forcing him to sit out for a period of time.

temper
A habit of getting angry quickly.

TO LEARN MORE

Books

Frederick, Jace. *Baseball's New Wave: The Young Superstars Taking Over the Game*. Mendota Heights, MN: Press Room Editions, 2019.

Gigliotti, Jim. *San Diego Padres*. Mankato, MN: The Child's World, 2019.

Mitchell, Bo. *Ultimate MLB Road Trip*. Minneapolis: Abdo Publishing, 2019.

Websites

Machado's Career Stats
https://www.baseball-reference.com/players/m/machama01.shtml

Machado's MLB Bio
https://www.mlb.com/player/manny-machado-592518

Padres Official Site
https://www.mlb.com/padres

INDEX